Welcome Home Swallows

HEIAN

FOR MY MOTHER, MISAKO SHIGEKAWA, MY HUSBAND, GENE GODIN, MY DAUGHTER, QUINCY GODIN AND IN MEMORY OF MY FATHER, KIYOSHI SHIGEKAWA.

MARLENE SHIGEKAWA

TO MY FAMILY. *ISAO KIKUCHI*

©2001 Text by Marlene Shigekawa / Illustrations by Isao Kikuchi

HEIAN INTERNATIONAL, INC.
1815 West 205th Street, Suite #301
Torrance, CA 90501

First American Edition 2001
10 9 8 7 6 5 4 3 2 1

Web Site: www.heian.com
E-mail: heianemail@heian.com

ISBN: 0-89346-934-3

Printed in Singapore

Welcome Home Swallows

Written by Marlene Shigekawa   **Illustrated by Isao Kikuchi**

4

For three years, Junior had longed to return home to Anaheim, California. But now that he was at home, he wasn't sure what to expect. He was certainly glad to be rid of the fierce desert winds that blew sand into his face and twirled him around like a tumbleweed. This was what he remembered most about living in the Poston, Arizona internment camp. His family was forced to live there by the United States government because the United States was at war with Japan and because they were Japanese.

Home at last, Junior's heart sang with joy. But the thought of attending a new school filled with strangers frightened him.

"I'll just have to be brave like Grandpa told me to be," he thought.

The next day, when Junior walked into his classroom, Mrs. Rainey, his teacher, welcomed him.

"Come right in and take a seat. You can sit here in front of Peter. He'll be your buddy today. Won't you, Peter?" asked Mrs. Rainey. Junior stared at Peter's hair that was as golden as a lion's mane.

"Yes, we can play together at recess," said Peter. Junior felt less scared.

During recess, Junior was busy playing marbles with Peter.
Then Bobby, another classmate, scowled and interrupted their game by
kicking the marbles and throwing dust at them.

"What are you doing?" shouted Peter.

"Why are you playing with him? He is not American," Bobby
replied angrily.

"I am too!" cried Junior.

"I can play with Junior if I want to," Peter said.
Then the bell rang and put a stop to the argument.

In class, Mrs. Rainey announced, "Next month we're going on a special field trip by bus to Mission San Juan Capistrano. The swallows fly 6000 miles each spring to return to the mission to build their nests. We're going to greet them when they return!"

Junior raised his hand. "Is the mission their home?" he asked. "Actually, they have two homes—one in Argentina where they go in the fall and another in San Juan Capistrano. They fly south for the winter to keep warm," explained Mrs. Rainey.

After school, Junior told his mother and grandpa as they drove home, "My class is going on a field trip to Mission San Juan Capistrano to see the swallows come home."

"How wonderful," his mother said. "Uncle Willie will be coming home soon too, just like the swallows."

"I can't wait to see him! And when will Uncle Min come home?"

"Let's not talk about Uncle Min," said Grandpa.

"Why not?" asked Junior.

Nobody answered Junior's questions, but he made a secret wish for both his uncles to come home soon.

11

Finally, the day of the field trip arrived. When Junior and his classmates reached the mission made of adobe bricks, they heard the bells ringing to welcome the swallows home. Some children were singing a song called "La Golondrina" which means swallow in Spanish. Mrs. Rainey gave everyone a generous handful of birdseed. All of Junior's classmates—except for Bobby—clustered together in the courtyard and searched the sky for the homeward-bound swallows. Junior watched Bobby as he frowned, threw away his birdseed, stomped over to a bench and sat down, all alone. Junior wondered why.

13

14

Suddenly, Junior heard the fluttering of wings. He saw birds high in the sky. "So these are the swallows of Mission San Juan Capistrano," he thought. Then he shouted, "Whee!" Delighted, he threw the birdseed up into the air. A single seed fell on Mrs. Rainey's head, and a swallow landed on it, trying to get the seed. Junior and Peter doubled over with laughter, and Mrs. Rainey chuckled as well. All of the children were laughing—except for Bobby. He just sat sadly on the bench with his arms folded across his chest.

The next day at school, Mrs. Rainey asked everyone to think about how to welcome someone home. "How did the people at San Juan Capistrano welcome the swallows?"

"They rang the mission bells," said Peter.

"They sang a song in Spanish," said Junior.

"Yes, there were many ways in which the swallows were welcomed home. Can you think about someone you would like to welcome home? I'd like you to draw a picture of what you would do to welcome someone special," said Mrs. Rainey.

As Junior drew, he thought about his secret wish that both his uncles would come home soon. After the students were finished, Peter was first to share his drawing.

"This is my dad coming home from the Navy. He's getting off a big ship, and the band is playing. I threw confetti to welcome him home."

Junior then wanted to share his picture. "This is my whole family having dinner after both my Uncle Willie and Uncle Min have come home. I made this "Welcome Home" sign hanging on the wall. It has stars and stripes on it."

"Bobby, why don't you share your drawing?" asked Mrs. Rainey.

"This is a drawing of my mom crying. She's crying because my dad is never coming home. He was killed in the war."

"Oh, Bobby—we are very sorry that your father died in the war. I'm sure that he was very brave—just as brave as you are today to share your drawing," said Mrs. Rainey.

After school, Junior invited Peter to his home. He showed Peter his treasure chest filled with special gifts--his rock collection, marbles, and a blue jay that Grandpa had carved in camp. Then he held up a photograph of Uncle Willie in his Army uniform,

"Is your Uncle Willie an American?" asked Peter.

"Yes, he went away to Italy to fight in the war," explained Junior.

"Oh, just like my dad," replied Peter.

Then Junior showed Peter a photograph of Uncle Min wearing a headband and a Japanese jacket called a "happi" coat.

"Did your Uncle Min go away to fight in the war too?" asked Peter.

"No, he just went away. Nobody will tell me where he is," Junior explained.

"Is he a Jap?" blurted Peter.

Startled, Junior said, "No, he isn't. And you shouldn't say that word!"

"Why not?" asked Peter.

"Because it makes me feel bad."

"But I didn't mean to make you feel bad," said Peter.

"Then don't ever say that again."

"Okay," replied Peter.

They were quiet for a few minutes until Peter asked, "Are you American like me?"

"Yes, I'm an American," Junior answered. "I was born right here in Anaheim. My grandparents came from Japan a long time ago."

"Are you sure you're an American?" Peter asked.

"Yes, I am sure," said Junior.

21

22

At school the next day, Junior and Peter were playing marbles during recess when Bobby walked over. He surprised them with his question.

"Are you a Jap?" Bobby asked Junior.

"Don't say that word. It makes him feel bad," said Peter.

"Well, nobody cares that I feel bad. Nobody cares that my dad died," said Bobby.

"That's not true! I care! I care because I know how much I miss my uncles! Do you want to play marbles with us?" asked Junior.

Bobby looked up and smiled at Junior for the first time. The three boys played together like old friends, and Peter said, "Junior is an American!"

Many days had passed since Junior's visit to Mission San Juan Capistrano. One day when his mother and his grandpa drove up to the school, Junior saw someone sitting in the back of the car. It was Uncle Willie! He stepped out of the car and gave Junior a warm hug.

"You finally came back!" Junior shouted. Then he noticed that Uncle Willie had hugged him with only one arm. His left arm was missing.

"What happened to your arm?" Junior asked.

"I lost it in the war," Uncle Willie explained.

"Were you in the hospital?"

"Yes, I was," said Uncle Willie.

"Well, at least you have your other arm," Junior said.

The following morning Junior and Uncle Willie practiced judo just as they had in Poston.

"Why did you go into the Army?" asked Junior. Uncle Willie paused and then said, "Because I wanted to show everyone that we are loyal Americans. We may look Japanese on the outside, but we're Americans in our hearts.

I thought that if I fought in the war, other people would see that we really are Americans. Then we could all return home and be together with our families."

Junior listened. "So you went to fight in the war to show other people that we're good Americans."

"Yes," said Uncle Willie, nodding his head.

Junior felt proud.

On the last day of school, when Junior arrived home, he saw someone sitting on the couch. It was Uncle Min! Junior ran to him for a big hug.

"It's so good to see you again,"
said Uncle Min.

"I didn't think you would ever come back.
Did you go to Japan? "

"No, but I wanted to," said Uncle Min."Did you fight against America?" asked Junior.

Uncle Min took a deep breath and said, "No, I didn't. I just spent time at Tule Lake, thinking about our family and thinking about the war."

"Do you like America better than Japan?" asked Junior.

"Do you like your mother better than your father?" asked Uncle Min.

"I love them both the same," Junior replied.

Uncle Min explained, "That's how I feel, too. I love both America and Japan."

Uncle Min and Junior then sat down at the dinner table with the whole family—Uncle Willie, Grandma and Grandpa, and Junior's mother and father and sister.

Junior thought a few minutes about what Uncle Min had said. Then he remembered that the swallows also had two homes and loved both places.

Beaming, he said, "Uncle Min, Uncle Willie—at last, you have come home just like the swallows at Mission San Juan Capistrano. Welcome home!"

Epilogue

(Note to Parents & Teachers)

During World War II, the U.S. government drafted interned Japanese American men. This action caused disagreement and division within many families. Some men who wished to demonstrate their loyalty to the United States volunteered for the famous 442nd Army Battalion, the most decorated unit of its size.

Others chose to demonstrate their rights by refusing to volunteer for the 442nd. They believed that it was unfair for them to be drafted by the government while their families were being held in internment camps. The U.S. government considered this group to be disloyal. Some men were sent to the "segregation" camp at Tule Lake, California. Some renounced their citizenship and went to Japan.

When the draft for Japanese Americans was reinstated, those who resisted the draft were sent to prison. The imprisoned men were released after the war ended, and President Harry Truman later pardoned them. Those Japanese Americans who had renounced their citizenship were eventually able to regain it.

Welcome Home, Swallows is the story of one Japanese American family that was able to reunite after the war ended.